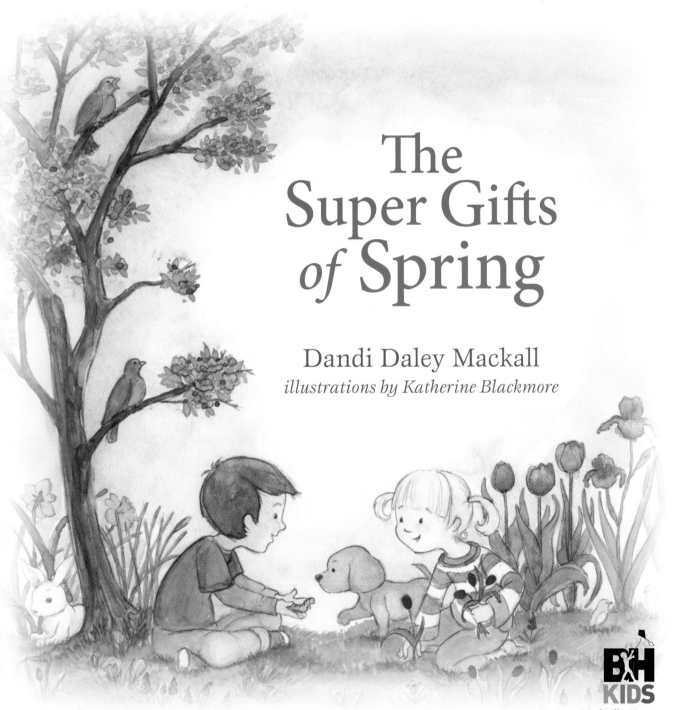

The
Super Gifts
of Spring

Dandi Daley Mackall

illustrations by Katherine Blackmore

B&H KIDS

Nashville, Tennessee

Dewey Decimal Classification: J508.2
Subject Heading: SPRING \ SEASONS \
EASTER

ISBN: 978-1-4336-8233-9
Printed in China
1 2 3 4 5 6 7 8 - 19 18 17 16 15

Let us strive to know the LORD. His appearance is as sure as the dawn.
He will come to us like the rain, like the spring showers that water the land.
—HOSEA 6:3

God created everything—
Summer, autumn, winter, spring.
See what springtime blessings bring. . . .
Thank You, God, for spring!

Look out, clouds! Here comes the sun!
See that rainbow, everyone?
Maybe winter's finally done.
Thank You, God, for spring.

"Whenever the rainbow appears in the clouds, I will see it and remember the everlasting covenant between God and all living creatures of every kind on the earth."—GENESIS 9:16 NIV

Ice is melting! Bubbling brook—
Time for fishing. Got your hook?
Spring is everywhere you look.
Thank You, God, for spring.

He causes the springs to gush into the valleys;
they flow between the mountains.
—Psalm 104:10

A *chick-chick-chick-chick*-chickadee
Is *tweet, tweet, tweet*-ing from a tree.
I hear that song You sent for me.
Thank You, God, for spring.

Even the stork in the sky knows her seasons.
The turtledove, swallow, and crane are aware of their migration.
—Jeremiah 8:7

Play outside now? Pretty please?
Splash in puddles. Feel that breeze?
Humming birds and buzzing bees—
Thank You, God, for spring.

He sends his word and melts them;
he stirs up his breezes, and the waters flow.
—PSALM 147:18 NIV

Follow *croak*-ing, find a toad.
Hurry, turtle! Cross the road.
Pigeons walking pigeon-toed.
Thank you, God, for spring.

The life of every living thing is in His hand,
as well as the breath of all mankind.
—JOB 12:10

Thanks for sending April showers,
Green, green grass and red, red flowers.
I can ride my bike for hours!
Thank You, God, for spring.

Sing to the LORD . . . who covers the sky with clouds, prepares
rain for the earth, and causes grass to grow on the hills.
—PSALM 147:7–8

I smell blessings after rain.
Wildflowers waving down the lane—
Give my mom a daisy chain.
Thank You, God, for spring.

"And why do you worry about clothes? Learn how the wildflowers
of the field grow: they don't labor or spin thread. Yet I tell you that
not even Solomon in all his splendor was adorned like one of these!"
—Matthew 6:28–29

Hug a puppy! Pet a bunny!
Days are getting very sunny.
Brand-new foal looks pretty funny.
Thank You, God, for spring.

How countless are Your works, LORD! In wisdom You have
made them all; the earth is full of Your creatures.
—PSALM 104:24

Dandelions turn to fluff.
Daddy says we have enough.
Still, it's fun to blow this stuff.
Thank You, God, for spring.

My soul, praise the LORD, and do not forget all His benefits.
—PSALM 103:2

Springtime! Great time! Check that date!
Know what's coming? I can't wait.
Easter! Time to celebrate.
Thank You, God, for spring.

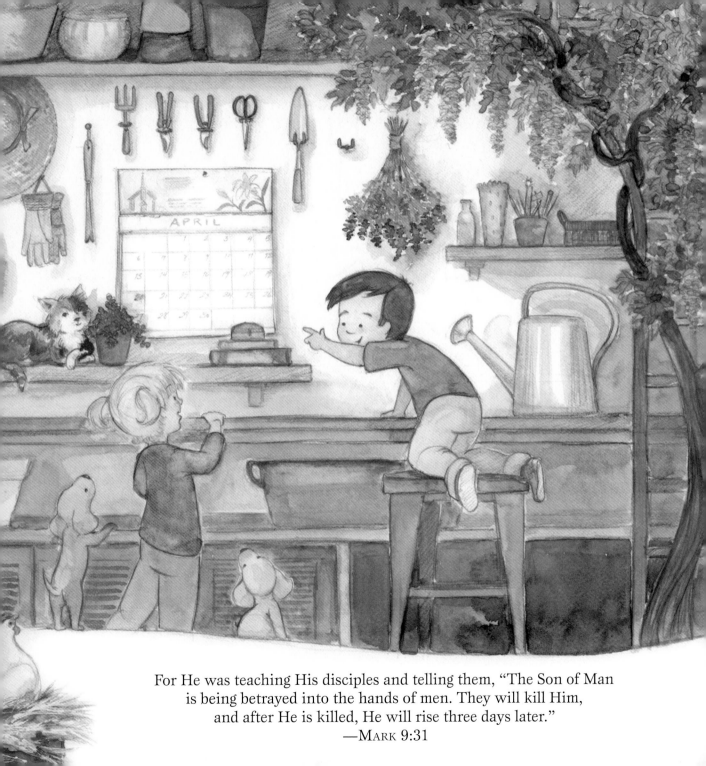

For He was teaching His disciples and telling them, "The Son of Man is being betrayed into the hands of men. They will kill Him, and after He is killed, He will rise three days later."
—MARK 9:31

Jesus gave His life for *you*.
What an awesome thing to do!
Rose again! Made all things new.
Thank You, God, for Jesus!

But now Christ has been raised from the dead. . . . For since death came through a man, the resurrection of the dead also comes through a man.
—1 Corinthians 15:20–21

Jesus lives! Now there's no doubt.
"Resurrection!" Shout it out.
That's what Easter's all about.
Thank You, God, for Easter!

Jesus said to her, "I am the resurrection and the life.
The one who believes in Me, even if he dies, will live."
—JOHN 11:25

Summer's just around the bend,
Filled with treasures God will send.
Spring is spinning to an end.
Thank You, God, for spring.

May the name of God be praised forever and ever, for wisdom and power
belong to Him. He changes the times and seasons.
—DANIEL 2:20–21

Remember:

Then the One seated on the throne said, "Look! I am making everything new."
—REVELATION 21:5

Read:

In Genesis 1, we see God filling the universe with new creations—a new sun and land, new plants and animals, and brand new people! Everything was shiny and unbroken; the world was perfect. But our world isn't perfect anymore, and sometimes you might find yourself wishing that sad or hard things in your life could be fresh and shiny instead. Every spring, God shows us that He continues to make things new. Green grass begins to grow once again, and tiny baby animals come into the world. Even more important, spring is a perfect time to celebrate the Resurrection of Jesus—by following Him, our hearts and lives can be made new too!

Think:

1. Why do you think God made four different seasons?
2. What are your favorite things about spring?
3. What Easter traditions do you have in your family? Which tradition do you enjoy the most?
4. Make a list with four columns: Write down the things you can see, touch, hear, and smell when springtime comes.
5. In spring, we enjoy new life such as baby animals and blooming flowers. Why is spring a perfect time to celebrate Jesus' resurrection too?

Do:

Grow a spring garden—in a cup!

1. On the side of a large Styrofoam cup, write: "Look! I am making everything new." —REVELATION 21:5
2. Decorate the rest of the cup with markers and stickers.
3. Fill the cup with potting soil.
4. Add a small amount of grass seed, and push the seeds gently into the soil. Water lightly.
5. Find two small twigs, and tie them together to make a cross. Place the base of the cross into the soil.
6. Wait for God to make the spring grass grow under the cross, reminding you of new life at Easter!

God is good at making all things new.